Cuando alguien tiene miedo

When Someone is Afraid

de/By Valeri Gorbachev
Ilustrado por/Illustrated by Kostya Gorbachev

STAR BRIGHT BOOKS
CAMBRIDGE MASSACHUSETTS

NOV 2017

First Spanish/English bilingual edition.
Published by Star Bright Books in 2016.

Copyright © 2005 Valeri Gorbachev.
Art copyright © 2005 Kostya Gorbachev.
Spanish text copyright © 2016 Star Bright Books.

All rights reserved. No part of this book may be reproduced or transmitted in any form or by any means that are available now or in the future without permission in writing from the copyright holders and the publisher.

The name Star Bright Books and the Star Bright Books logo are registered trademarks of Star Bright Books, Inc. Please visit www.starbrightbooks.com.
For bulk orders, please email: orders@starbrightbooks.com, or call (617) 354-1300.

Translated by Eida del Risco

Spanish/English Bilingual Paperback ISBN: 978-1-59572-744-2
Star Bright Books/MA/00103160
Printed in China (WKT) 9 8 7 6 5 4 3 2 1

Printed on paper from sustainable forests.

Library of Congress Cataloging-in-Publication Data is available.

Cuando un avestruz tiene miedo...
hunde la cabeza en la arena.

When an ostrich is afraid. . .
it buries its head in the sand.

Cuando una jirafa tiene miedo...
huye lo más rápido que puede.

When a giraffe is afraid. . .
it runs away as fast as it can.

Cuando los peces tienen miedo...
... salen disparados como flechas.

When fish are afraid. . .
they dart away.

Cuando las ranas tienen miedo...
se zambullen en la charca.

When frogs are afraid. . .
they dive into a pond.

Cuando los cuervos tienen miedo...
se alejan volando.

When crows are afraid. . .
they fly away.

Cuando un conejo tiene miedo...
corre hacia los arbustos.

When a rabbit is afraid. . .
it races into the bushes.

Cuando una tortuga tiene miedo...
... se encoge dentro del caparazón.

When a turtle is afraid. . .
it shrinks into its shell.

Cuando una ardilla tiene miedo...
... sube a un árbol a toda velocidad.

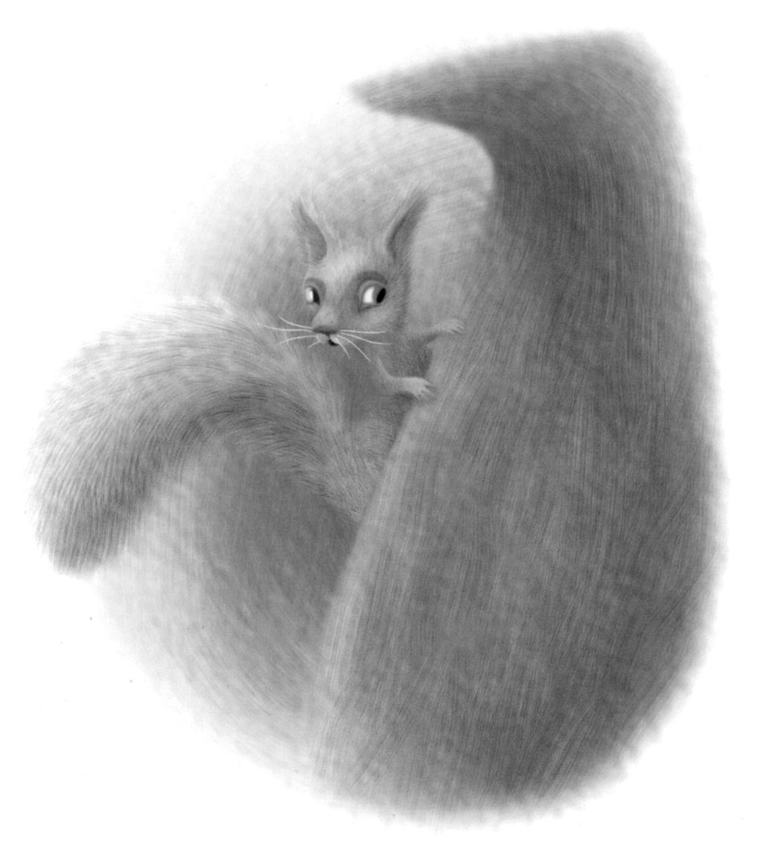

When a squirrel is afraid. . .
it scampers up a tree.

Cuando un ratón tiene miedo...
se mete en un agujero.

When a mouse is afraid. . .
it hurries into a hole.

Cuando mi gato tiene miedo…
se esconde bajo mi cama.

When my kitten is afraid. . .
she hides under my bed.

Cuando mi perro tiene miedo...
se esconde detrás de mí.

When my dog is afraid. . .
he hides behind me.

Cuando yo tengo miedo…
llamo a mamá o a papá.

When I get scared,
I call Mommy or Daddy.

—¡Mamá!
"MOMMY!"

—¿Qué pasa, cariño?

"What's wrong, honey?"

–Tuve una
pesadilla.

"I had a
bad dream."

Mamá me da un abrazo…

Mommy gives me a hug. . .

y un beso…

and a kiss. . .

y se me quita el miedo.

and I am not afraid anymore.